USBORNE ENGLISH

SPELLING PUZZLES

Jenny Tyler, Robyn Gee and Peter McClelland

Designed and illustrated by

Graham Round

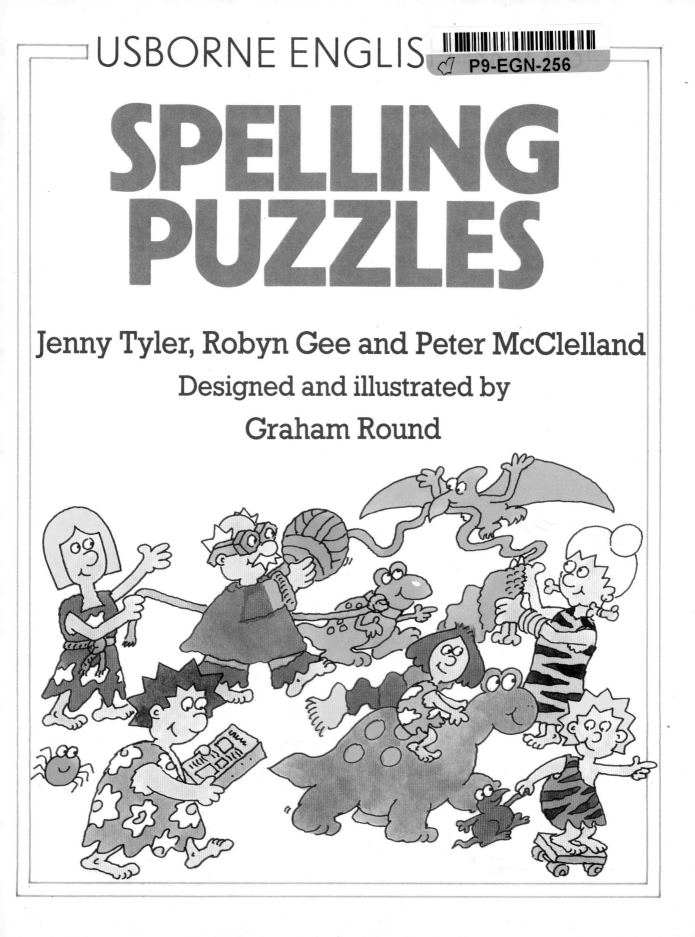

How to use this book

In this book you will find lots of puzzles which will help you to think about words and how to write them.

The answers to the puzzles are at the back of the book on pages 26 to 29. When you don't know an answer, try to guess what it could be before looking it up in the back, or asking someone else to help you.

> It's always a good idea to try and guess.

If you know an answer but don't know how to spell it there is a spellcheck list on page 32, where you can look it up before writing it down.

The spellcheck list is in alphabetical order, like a dictionary. When two words begin with the same letter, the word whose second letter is first in the alphabet comes first.

apples
basket
bear

> "Basket" comes before "bear" because "a" comes before "e".

Some of the pages may give you ideas for making up your own word games to play with a friend. You could muddle up the letters in words, like the ones on the signs on pages 8 and 9, and then see whether your friend could sort them into the right order. You might have to give a clue about what the word means. Or you could make up word quizzes for each other, like the one on pages 18 and 19.

Hints on learning to spell

When you are learning how to spell a word, follow the four steps below:

Step 1
LOOK at the word carefully. Notice the order of the letters. Say the letters to yourself a few times. Pretend to write it with your finger.

Step 2
COVER the word with a piece of scrap paper, so that you can't see it.

Step 3
WRITE it down from memory. It is important to write the word down, rather than just looking at it, or saying it aloud. The way your hand moves when

you are writing, will help your brain to remember the shape of the word.

Step 4
CHECK that it is right. If it is wrong, cover it up and start again, paying particular attention to the letters you got wrong.

You need a good, clear dictionary to help you check your spellings. If you are not sure how to find the words you want, ask someone to explain to you exactly how to use it.

Always read through what you have written and check any words you are unsure of in your dictionary.

Break longer words up into separate sounds or syllables, instead of thinking of one long string of letters.

Introducing Ogtown

In this book you will meet a family called the Ogs. This picture map shows part of Ogtown, where they live. Can you fill in the letters missing from the names on the map?

Va_le_ of Moss

Painted c_v_s

Ichthyosaur la__

The Og's hou_e

Ogtown s__ool

Rose ri_e_

Stegosaurus str__t

Pet s__p

Bonehead li__ary

Reptile r__d

3

Meet the Og family

Grandma Og

Grandma Og spends all her time knitting clothes. When she writes, she puts the wrong letter at the beginning of every word.

Grandpa Og

Grandpa Og enjoys dancing. He is specially fond of heavy rock music. When he writes he leaves out the first letter of every word.

Mrs. Og

Mrs. Og loves animals. Her hobby is breeding dinosaurs. She writes the wrong letter before the last letter of every word.

Mr. Og

Mr. Og is the cook of the family. He makes delicious sausages. He also brews his own wines from wild plants. He always writes the wrong letter at the end of words.

Mog Og

Mog Og is the school skipping champion. She is a very fast runner as well. She keeps putting the letter "s" in places where it doesn't belong.

Zog Og

Zog Og goes everywhere by skateboard and is a fan of the famous pop star, Damonna. He writes a "d" instead of the first letter of every word.

The Ogs often leave stone notes for each other. Can you work out which member of the family wrote each of these notes? Can you write down in their speech bubbles what they meant to say?

Invitation to a picnic

The Ogs have received an invitation to a picnic from their friends, the Igs. Unfortunately all the vowels on the Igs' typewriter have worn out. Can you fill in the vowels to complete the invitation?

The vowels are a, e , i o and u.

Th_ Igs _nv_t_ th_ Og f_m_ly t_ th__r p_cn_c _n th_ f__rth d_y _f th_ n_w m__n _t m_dd_y
Pl__s_ br_ng s_m_ f__d _nd dr_nk

The Ogs wrote back, saying they would love to come. They sent a list of the food they would take with them. Can you fill in the missing letters to find out what they planned to bring?

Each food on the list should have a double letter in it.

Can you think of any more foods with double letters in them?

ch__se   a__les
bu__er   strawbe__ies
co__ee   le__uce
ca__ots   e__s

The picnic map

This is the map the Igs sent with their invitation. The last letter of each place on the map is missing. Each of the missing letters is one of the points of the compass (that is n, s, e or w). Having filled in the last letter of the first place, the Ogs should go in that direction until they reach another place and so on. Make sure you go in a straight line from one place to another. Where is the great picnic to be held?

At the market

Mog and Mr. Og have come to the market to buy the things they need for the picnic. They are having difficulty finding the things they want because the letters on the signs are all jumbled up. Can you sort out the letters to find out what each stall sells? Use the pictures to help you.

crocodile eatm

hewels

vetegables truif

syot

pet doof

bedra

caterllipar maj

wenspareps

frish fesh

lossifs

9

Grandma Og's recipes

Grandma Og gets out some recipes for Mog and Zog to make. They are so old that the letters are wearing away in places. Help Mog and Zog to understand what to do by filling in the missing letters.

Stone buns

Ingredients:

flo__r   s__g__r

n__ts   m__rg__rine

c__rr__nts   golden syr__p

W__rm m__rg__rine __nd syr__p

Mix well __nd p__t a te__spoonf__l

of the mixt__re on a b__king sheet

B__ke for fo__rteen min__tes

The missing letters are all "u"s and "a"s.

yum yum juice

Ingredients: tw__ ba__a__as

o__e sp____ful of __ra__ge jelly

two teasp____s h____ey

o__e pi__t c__ld milk

Mash ba__a__as in a b__wl

Add jelly a__d h____ey

Ble__d i__ milk

One missing letter is "n", what is the other?

10

Cooking for the picnic

The whole Og family is busy cooking things for the picnic. Fill in the missing words to show what everyone is doing.

The list of words below may help you think of the right word to fit each space.

bake   weigh
spread   lick
break   taste
    grate

I'm _____ a cake

I'm _____ an egg

I'm _____ the sugar

I'm _____ the cheese

I'm _____ the soup

I'm _____ the spoon

I'm _____ the butter

You have to add "ing" to the end of the words to make them fit.

For words ending in "e", take off the "e" before you add "ing".

Picnic games

Spotters' challenge

When the Ogs and the Igs finished their picnic, Grandpa Og organized a spotting game.

He thought of ten things that everybody had to find. Then he cut each word into two parts and arranged all the pieces in a spider's web pattern. Can you match the pairs to find out what they had to spot?

lady
hopper
earth
dragon
dil

pede
fly
wood
tad
fly

pole
grass
pecker
toad
bird

worm
daffo
butter
stool
centi

Word Search

The Igs have challenged the Ogs to a game of word search. They have written words on their empty picnic plates. Each of the words can make a new word by changing the order of the letters. Can you help the Ogs to find the new words? You must use all the letters in the word to make the new word.

Write your list on the orange lines.

Something you sit on.

east

fare

Move the "e".

Not right.

grown

inch

Keep the "ch" together.

Baby animal

loaf

rinse

Emergency vehicles use one.

Stone rolling

Zog has found lots of round stones and written letters on them. He has built a run for them with his spade. At the bottom of the run is a big stone with "sh" on it.

Can you help the others choose two stones at a time to roll down the run to make up ten different four letter words that end in "sh"?

a d i
w i f d a r
a u u i s a
p w a r c

sh

Find your way around Ogtown

Which ending goes with "st" to mean not fresh?
1. ake 2. alk
3. ale

3 2 1

Which word is a shiny metal.?
1. steal
2. stole
3. steel

1 2 3

One day Mr. and Mrs. Ig decide to give Tig and Mig a treat after school. Tig and Mig don't know where they are going, but they have to follow a trail left by their parents. Mr. and Mrs. Ig have left question clues at each junction they will come to.

Every time they come to a road junction they have to choose the best answer to the question and follow the direction indicated by the number of the correct answer. Can you draw in a line to show the route they should take? What is the treat?

In which word can the letters be rearranged to show what you produce when you cry?
1. star   2. stare   3. stay

Which word means a large animal?
1. beast
2. fast
3. feast

Which word is missing the letter "e"?
1. stream
2. style
3. strik

Space project

Mog's class at school is doing a project. Their teacher, Miss Spell, has asked them to imagine that one day people will be able to fly into space. She has then given them various tasks to do for the project.

Everyone has to write a newspaper article about flying into space. Mog has written about a rocket launch, but she is not sure which double letters to use in some of the words. Can you help her fill in the missing spaces?

The launch of the space shu__le Usbornus Thr__ was postponed because of te__ible thunderstorms today. Another a__empt is pla__ed for tomo__ow. Meanwhile the Ru__ians had a su__e__ful launch of their sate__ite at noon today.

Miss Spell, has made up a space code. In the code instead of C you write A, instead of D you write B, and so on.

How does the code work? Write the rest of the code letters under the alphabet below.

Can you decode each of the words Miss Spell has written on the board? Use the alphabet below to help you.

pmaicr

njylcr

yqrpmlysr

kyprgyl

amslrbmul

a b c d e f g h i j k l m n o p q r s t u v w x y z
a b

Miss Spell has asked everyone to write down six things that they would definitely take with them if they could go on a journey into space. Unfortunately Zog kept pressing the wrong keys on his wordprocessor while writing his list. Can you cross out the first letter of each word and write the correct letter above it, to find out what he wanted to take?

bam larts

thocolate tudge

reddy sear

men snife

gennis backet

romputer names

Make a path

Grandpa Og gave Grandma this game for her birthday. Have a go at playing it. Choose a yellow shape to start on. Read the clue inside it and write letters in the spaces to give the right answer. Then move to a shape that touches the one you started on. Keep moving to connecting shapes and writing the answers. The aim is to get from a yellow shape to a green shape in an unbroken path. If you move to a word you cannot spell, move back to the shape you have just done and then to another shape that touches it. When you have finished, check your answers in the back of the book. If your answer is right, use a crayon to fill in the shape. If your answer is wrong, see if you can fill in a connecting shape to keep your path unbroken.

po_ _ _ _
sharp end

s_ _ _ _
you use this to wash yourself

din_ _ _ _ _ _
ancient animal

l_ _ _ _
not tight

gr_ _ _ _ _
what's under your feet

fri_ _ _
someone you like and who likes you

u_ _ _ _ _ _
helpful

h_ _ _
sixty minutes

esc_ _ _ _
get free

18

mi _ _ _ _
sixty seconds

ju _ _ _
liquid in fruit

r _ _ _ _
opposite of left

v _ _ _ _
sound coming from mouth

no _ _ _
a sound, usually loud

kn _ _ _ _ _
part of your finger

w _ _ _ _ _ _
rain, snow, sun, ice fog

sc _ _ _
an animal's smell

of _ _ _
many times

cau _ _ _
trapped

is _ _ _ _
land surrounded by water

t _ _ _ _
not loose

c _ _ _ _
tells the time

y _ _ _
yellow part of an egg

The newspaper

The Og children have decided to start a newspaper for their family and friends. Roving reporters Zog Og and Tig Ig have been collecting news stories. They had to write so quickly that their news items contain some spelling mistakes. You can see their notebooks on these two pages.

See if you can find four spelling errors in each report. When you find a mistake, put a line through the whole word and write it correctly above. (Zog has already corrected one of his mistakes like this.)

"Toys Were Us" the mammoth new toy shop is having a fantastic sale of model erth ~~creetures~~ *creatures* this week. Speaars and tepots are also being sold at half price. Don't miss it.

The four words spelled wrong should all have "ea" in them.

The Big Rock Stadium was packt last night when the left-handid John Jelly set a new world record of four hundrod strides for middle-weight stone throwing. The crowd cheerd him off the ground.

The four words spelled wrong should all end in "ed".

For priceless tiger-tooth necklaces were stolen from the Ogtown undergrond car park late yesterday. Police have surrownded the area, but they still have not been fownd.

The Rocks performed their numbar one hit 'I can't get no brontosauri,' with incredible powerr at the Hilltop Arena last night. Lead singir Oggy Pip and drummear Yoggy Urt held the crowd spellbound.

The misspelled words should all have "ou" in them.

CAR PARK

The words spelled wrong should all end in "er".

21

Mog's photographs

Mog Og has taken some photos for the newspaper and written underneath each one. Her wordprocessor wasn't working properly and some of the words have all their letters mixed up. Can you find the mixed up words and write the correct word above each one? Use the pictures to help you.

A gradeb called Brian who eats twenty nasanab a day won the best pet competition

Sid Um, his arm still heavily andedbag talking today of how he caught the nitbad single-handed

All the words begin with "ba"

Wearing his best blabseal hat Uncle Ig shows off the Ogtown Bashers new club debag

22

Damonna's delights

Zog Og was thrilled to get an interview with the famous rockstar, Damonna, when she visited Ogtown. He wrote down Damonna's top ten things on his noterock, but he accidentally dropped and broke it on his way home. Can you help Zog to sort the broken pieces into pairs and list Damonna's top ten things below? Write one of them on each line.

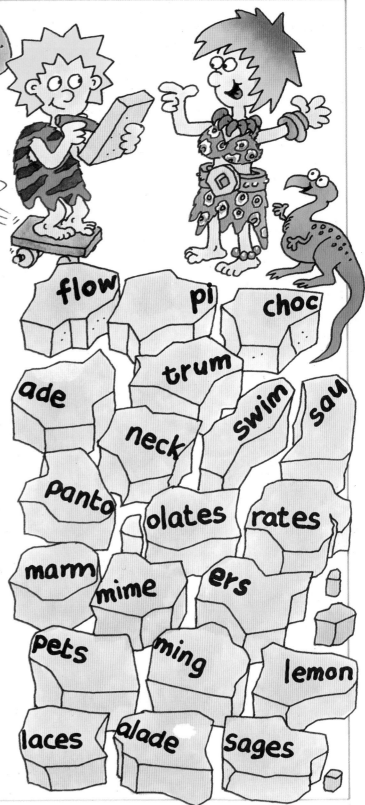

flow
pi
choc
trum
ade
neck
swim
sau
panto
olates
rates
marm
mime
ers
pets
ming
lemon
laces
alade
sages

Ogtown News

Here is a page from the first issue of the newspaper Mog has started with the help of her family and friends. She has checked it carefully, but she has confused some words with words that sound the same but are spelled differently. How many mistakes can you find? Put a line through each one as you find it. Try doing the crossword and the competitions as well.

The editorial team includes the following:
Zog Og (photographer)
Mig Ig (reporter)
Tig Ig (advertisements and competitions)
Grandma Og (editorial assistant and tea-maker).

A good reed

"The White Which" is a very exciting tail about a which who captured a bare and taught it to dance. In the end the which dyed.

Meat the editor

This is Mog Og, editor of your new weekly journal "The Ogtown News". We hope you will reed every issue and right and tell us what you think.

Whether report

Sunny at first with rein later in the day.

Windy at see. Where something warm.

Dates for your Diary

1 May Jumble sail in St Frogs Church Hall

4 May Nature ramble in the woulds.

20 May The Ogtown Bashers v. the Ugtown Mugs

Dear Mog,

I here you are starting a newspaper. What a good idea! I no it will be a success.

Grandpa Og

Crossword

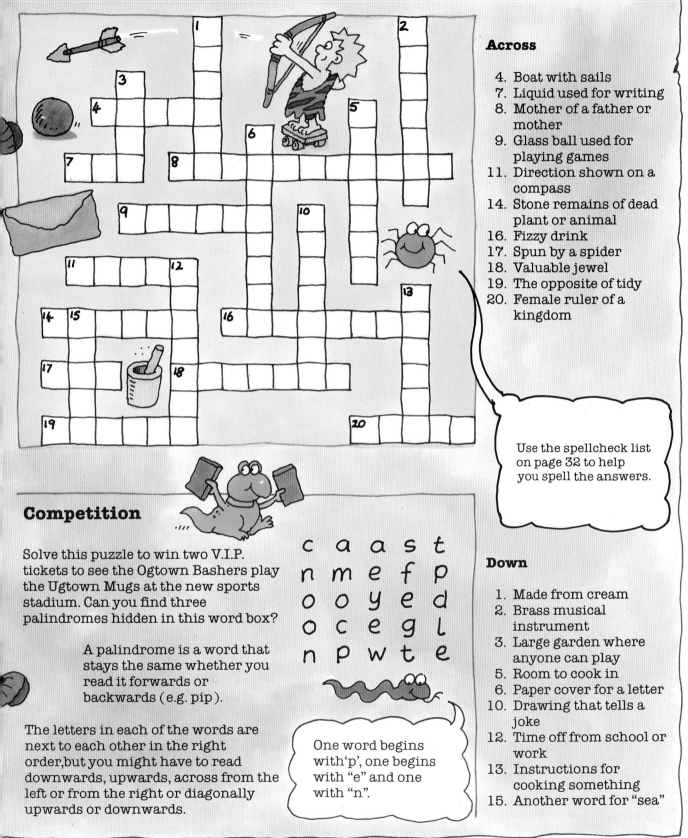

Use the spellcheck list on page 32 to help you spell the answers.

Across

4. Boat with sails
7. Liquid used for writing
8. Mother of a father or mother
9. Glass ball used for playing games
11. Direction shown on a compass
14. Stone remains of dead plant or animal
16. Fizzy drink
17. Spun by a spider
18. Valuable jewel
19. The opposite of tidy
20. Female ruler of a kingdom

Competition

Solve this puzzle to win two V.I.P. tickets to see the Ogtown Bashers play the Ugtown Mugs at the new sports stadium. Can you find three palindromes hidden in this word box?

A palindrome is a word that stays the same whether you read it forwards or backwards (e.g. pip).

The letters in each of the words are next to each other in the right order, but you might have to read downwards, upwards, across from the left or from the right or diagonally upwards or downwards.

```
c  a  a  s  t
n  m  e  f  p
o  o  y  e  d
o  c  e  g  l
n  p  w  t  e
```

One word begins with 'p', one begins with "e" and one with "n".

Down

1. Made from cream
2. Brass musical instrument
3. Large garden where anyone can play
5. Room to cook in
6. Paper cover for a letter
10. Drawing that tells a joke
12. Time off from school or work
13. Instructions for cooking something
15. Another word for "sea"

25

Spell for your Life

There are five vowels. They are the letters "a", "e", "i", "o" and "u".

A word is made up of one or more syllables or sounds

START

Spell the word....

Name the vowels in the word....

How many syllables are there in the word....?

Spell the word....

Spell the word....

Are there silent lett in the wo ....?

What are the first three letters of the word ....?

Which letter in the word .... comes first in the alphabet?

Grandpa Og has given Zog a game called "Spell for your Life" for his birthday.

You will need a dice, a counter and at least 20 pieces of paper large enough to write one word on. Get the spellmaster to write a word on each piece.*

The player starts with three lives. The aim of the game is to reach the finish and have an Ogburger. He puts his counter on "start" and throws the dice. He then moves forward the number of places shown on the dice. The spellmaster asks the question he lands on, using the top word in place of the dots.

If the player answers correctly, he throws again and moves on. If he gets it wrong, he loses a life and stays where he is to answer another question.

If a player loses three lives, he has to go back to the beginning and start again.

You may need to write the word down before answering the question.

"Plural" means "more than one". To make a word plural you usually add "s" or "es".

*She could choose these from the Spellcheck list on page 32.

Answers

Page 3

Page 5

Pages 8 and 9
At the market

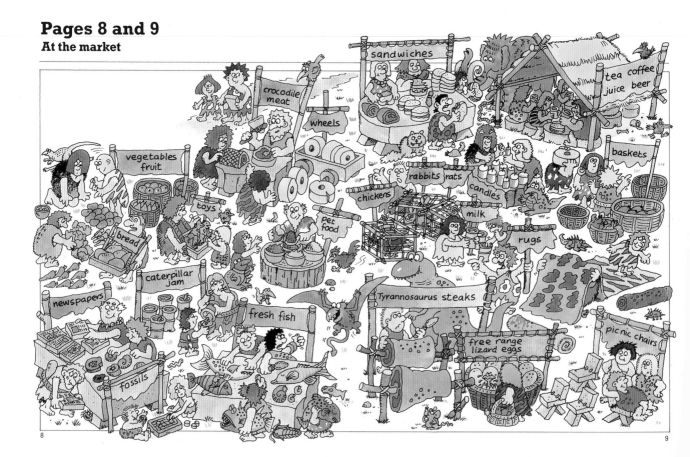

Has anyone seen my knitting needles?

My skateboard is broken.

Dinosaur chops for supper tonight.

Page 6

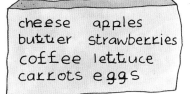

The Igs invite the Og family to their picnic on the fourth day of the new moon at midday. Please bring some food and drink.

cheese   apples
butter   strawberries
coffee   lettuce
carrots   eggs

Page 7

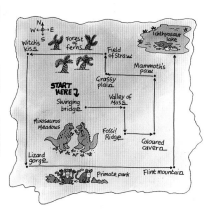

N W E S
Witch's kiss
Forest of ferns
Field of straw
Ichthyosaur lake
Mammoth's paw
START HERE
Grassy plain
Swinging bridge
Valley of Moss
Mixosaurus Meadows
Fossil Ridge
Coloured cavern
Lizard gorge
Primate park
Flint mountain

Page 10

Stone buns
Ingredients:
flour   sugar
nuts   margarine
currants   golden syrup

Warm margarine and syrup
Mix well and put a teaspoonful
of the mixture on a baking sheet
Bake for fourteen minutes

The missing letters are all "u"s and "a"s.

Yum yum juice
Ingredients: two bananas
one spoonful of orange jelly
two teaspoons honey
one pint cold milk
Mash bananas in a bowl
Add jelly and honey
Blend in milk

One missing letter is "n", what is the other?

Page 11

I'm baking a cake

I'm breaking an egg

I'm weighing the sugar

I'm grating the cheese

I'm tasting the soup

I'm licking the spoon

I'm spreading the butter

Page 12

1. ladybird
2. grasshopper
3. earthworm
4. dragonfly
5. daffodil
6. centipede
7. toadstool
8. woodpecker
9. butterfly
10. tadpole

Page 13

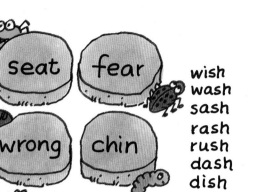

wish
wash
sash
rash
rush
dash
dish
cash
fish
push

Page 17

pmaicr — rocket
njylcr — planet
yqrpmlysr — astronaut
kyprgyl — martian
amslrbmul — countdown

jam tarts
chocolate fudge
teddy bear
pen knife
tennis racket
computer games

In the space code you count back 2 letters from the one you want to write

Pages 14 and 15

Find your way around Ogtown

Page 16

The launch of the space shuttle Usbornus Three was postponed because of terrible thunderstorms today. Another attempt is planned for tomorrow. Meanwhile the Russians had a successful launch of their satellite at noon today.

Pages 18 and 19

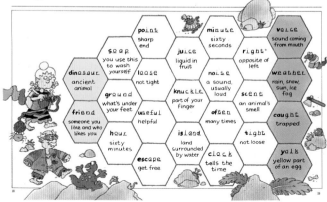

point — sharp end
minute — sixty seconds
voice — sound coming from mouth
soap — you use this to wash yourself
juice — liquid in fruit
right — opposite of left
dinosaur — ancient animal
loose — not tight
noise — a sound, usually loud
weather — rain, snow, sun, ice fog
ground — what's under your feet
knuckle — part of your finger
scent — an animal's smell
friend — someone you like and who likes you
useful — helpful
often — many times
caught — trapped
hour — sixty minutes
island — land surrounded by water
tight — not loose
yolk — yellow part of an egg
escape — get free
clock — tells the time

Pages 20 and 21

Note 1:
"Toys WereUs, the mammoth new toy shop is having a fantastic ~~erth creatures~~ earth creatures sale of model ~~Spears~~ this week. ~~Spears~~ Spears and ~~tepots~~ teapots are also being sold at half price. Don't miss it.

Note 2:
The Big Rock Stadium was ~~packt~~ packed last night when the left-handed ~~handid~~ handed John Jelly set a new world record of four ~~hundrod~~ hundred strides for middle-weight stone throwing. The crowd ~~cheerd~~ cheered him off the ground.

Note 3:
~~For~~ Four priceless tiger-tooth necklaces were stolen from the Ogtown ~~undergrond~~ underground car park late yesterday. Police have ~~surrownded~~ surrounded the area, but they still have not been ~~fownd~~ found.

Note 4:
The Rocks performed their ~~numbar~~ number one hit 'I can't get no brontosauri,' with incredible ~~powerk~~ power at the Hilltop Arena last night. Lead ~~singir~~ singer Oggy Pip and ~~drummear~~ drummer Yoggy Urt held the crowd spellbound.

Pages 22 and 23

A ~~gradeb~~ badger called Brian who eats twenty ~~nasanab~~ bananas a day won the best pet competition

Sid Um, his arm still heavily ~~andedbag~~ bandaged talking today of how he caught the ~~nit bad~~ bandit single-handed

Wearing his best ~~blabseal~~ baseball hat Uncle Ig shows off the Ogtown Bashers new club ~~debag~~ badge

1. flowers
2. pirates
3. chocolates
4. lemonade
5. trumpets
6. swimming
7. sausages
8. marmalade
9. necklaces
10. pantomime

Pages 24 and 25

Ogtown News

Here is a page from the first issue of the newspaper Mog has started with the help of her family and friends. She has checked it carefully, but she has confused some words that sound the same but are spelled differently. How many mistakes can you find? Put a line through each one as you find it. Try doing the crossword and the competitions as well.

The editorial team includes the following:
Zog Og (photographer)
Mig Ig (reporter)
Tig Ig (advertisements and competitions)
Grandma Og (editorial assistant and tea-maker).

A good ~~reed~~ read
"The White ~~Which~~ Witch" is a very exciting ~~taitale~~ tale about a ~~which~~ witch who ~~witch~~ captured a ~~bare~~ bear and taught it to dance. In the end the ~~which~~ witch ~~dyed~~ died

~~Meat~~ Meet the editor

This is Mog Og, editor of your new weekly journal "The Ogtown News". We hope you will ~~reed~~ read every issue and ~~right~~ write and tell us what you think.

~~Whether~~ Weather report

Sunny at first with ~~rein~~ rain later in the day.
Windy at ~~see~~ sea. ~~Where~~ Wear something warm.

Dates for your Diary

1 May Jumble ~~sail~~ sale in St Frogs Church Hall

4 May Nature ramble in the ~~woulds~~ woods

20 May The Ogtown Bashers v. the Ugtown Mugs

Letters to the editor

Dear Mog,
I ~~hare~~ hear you are starting a newspaper. What a good idea! I ~~no~~ know it will be a success.
Grandpa Og

Crossword

Across
4. Boat with sails
7. Liquid used for writing
8. Mother of a father or mother
9. Glass ball used for playing games
11. Direction shown on a compass
14. Stone remains of dead plant or animal
16. Fizzy drink
17. Spun by a spider
18. Valuable jewel
19. The opposite of tidy
20. Female ruler of a kingdom

Down
1. Made from cream
2. Brass musical instrument
3. Large garden where anyone can play
5. Room to cook in
6. Paper cover for a letter
10. Drawing that tells a joke
12. Time off from school or work
13. Instructions for cooking something
15. Another word for "sea"

Crossword answers shown: YACHT, INK, GRANDMOTHER, MARBLE, NORTH, FOSSIL, WEB, DIAMOND, UNTIDY, LEMONADE, QUEEN, TRUMPET, BUTTER, PARK, KITCHEN, ENVELOPE, CREAM, CARTOON, RECIPE

Use the spellcheck list on page 32 to help you spell the answers.

Competition

Solve this puzzle to win two V.I.P. tickets to see the Ogtown Bashers play the Ugtown Mugs at the new sports stadium. Can you find three palindromes hidden in this word box?

A palindrome is a word that stays the same whether you read it forwards or backwards (e.g. pip).

The letters in each of the words are next to each other in the right order, but you might have to read downwards, upwards, across from the left or from the right or diagonally upwards or downwards.

```
c a a s t
m e f p
o o y e d
o c e g l
h p w t e
```

One word begins with 'p', one begins with "e" and one with "n".

Spellcheck list

anyone
apples
asteroid
attempt
badge
badger
bake
baking
bananas
bandaged
bandit
baseball
baskets
bear
beer
blend
blue
bowl
bridge
broken
brown
butter
butterfly
candles
carrots
cartoon
caterpillar
caught
cavern
caves
centipede
cheered
cheese
chickens

chin
chocolate
clock
coffee
cold
computer
countdown
currants
daffodil
diamond
died
dinosaur
dragonfly
drummer
earth
earthworm
eggs
eight
envelope
escape
fear
fish
five
flour
foal
food
fossils
four
fourteen
fresh
friend
fruit
fudge
games

gorge
grandmother
grasshopper
ground
hear
holiday
honey
hour
hundred
ink
island
jam
juice
kiss
kitchen
knife
knitting
know
knuckle
ladybird
lake
left-handed
lemonade
lettuce
library
lizard
loose
marble
marmalade
margarine
Martian
meat
meet
milk

minutes
mixture
moss
mountain
necklaces
needles
newspapers
nine
noise
noon
north
number
nuts
one
packed
pantomimes
park
paw
pen
picnic
pie
pink
pint
pirates
plain
planet
planned
power
queue
rabbits
racket
rain
rats
read

recipe
ridge
right
river
road
rocket
round
rugs
Russians
sale
sandwiches
satellite
sausages
school
scent
sea
seat
shop
shuttle
singer
siren
six
skateboard
soap
spears
steaks
straw
strawberries
street
successful
sugar
supper
surrounded
swimming

syrup
tadpole
tale
tea
teapots
tears
teaspoon
teaspoonful
teddy
tennis
terrible
three
tight
toadstool
tomorrow
tonight
trumpets
two
underground
valley
volcano
warm
wear
weather
web
wheels
white
witch
woodpecker
woods
write
wrong
yacht
yellow